THE FARMER IN THE DELL

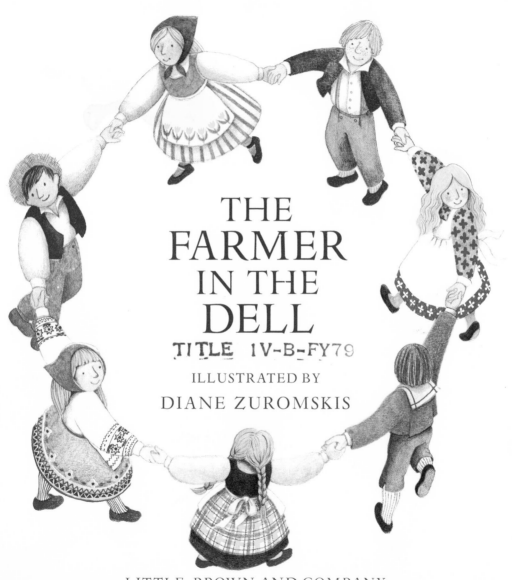

THE
FARMER
IN THE
DELL

TITLE IV-B-FY79

ILLUSTRATED BY

DIANE ZUROMSKIS

LITTLE, BROWN AND COMPANY

BOSTON   TORONTO

FIRST EDITION

T 03/78

Library of Congress Cataloging in Publication Data

Main entry under title:

The Farmer in the dell.

  SUMMARY: A traditional American singing game
about a farmer and what happens when he takes a wife.
  [1. Folk songs. 2. Singing games] I. Zuromskis,
Diane.
PZ8.3.F2285   784.4   77–17074
ISBN 0–316–98889–8

*Published simultaneously in Canada
by Little, Brown & Company (Canada) Limited*

PRINTED IN THE UNITED STATES OF AMERICA

For Katie and Tamara

The farmer in the dell,
The farmer in the dell,

Hi-ho the Derry-o,
The farmer in the dell.

The farmer takes a wife,

The farmer takes a wife,

Hi-ho the Derry-o,
The farmer takes a wife.

The wife takes a child,
The wife takes a child,
Hi-ho the Derry-o,
The wife takes a child.

The child takes a nurse,
The child takes a nurse,
Hi-ho the Derry-o,
The child takes a nurse.

The nurse takes a dog,
The nurse takes a dog,
Hi-ho the Derry-o,
The nurse takes a dog.

The dog takes a cat,
The dog takes a cat,
Hi-ho the Derry-o,
The dog takes a cat.

The cat takes a rat,
The cat takes a rat,
Hi-ho the Derry-o,
The cat takes a rat.

The rat takes the cheese,
The rat takes the cheese,
Hi-ho the Derry-o,
The rat takes the cheese.

The cheese stands alone,
The cheese stands alone,
Hi-ho the Derry-o,
The cheese stands alone.